CAMPING
WITH
ELLEN Grape

ANgie ELLiSON

To order additional copies of this book, contact:
Xlibris
844-714-8691
www.Xlibris.com
Orders@Xlibris.com

ISBN: Softcover   978-1-6698-7070-8
         Hardcover   978-1-6698-7071-5
         EBook   978-1-6698-7069-2

Print information available on the last page

Rev. date: 03/14/2023

CAMPING
with
ELLEN Grape

Hi, my name is Ellen Grape
Let's go camping
By the lake

Setting up our tent
Is the first thing we do
Here are the stakes
For you and me

4

Making, it straight
Sturdy and strong
With a hammer and hard work
We can't go wrong

Some tents are green
Mine is red
With blankets and pillows
It's a perfect bed

Dallis, my best friend
Came with me
We're gathering branches
That fell from a tree

Trails we can hike
Or ride a bike
Exploring nature
Is what I like

Watching birds high
In the trees
My pink binoculars
Are special to me

My favorite game
The sleeping bag race
Last one to finish
Gets a pie in the face

A day of fun
Swimming and canoeing
Eating and laughing
At what everyone's doing

18

We chose our favorite
Fishing spot
As you can see
We caught a lot

I caught five
Dallis has three
Worms are slimy
And ikky to me

worm

23

Special bracelets
We made together
Being best friends
Like birds of a feather

25

Dad made a campfire
Now that it's dark
Scary ghost stories
Are sure to start

Have you ever made
S'mores before?
I have my recipe
Great for outdoors

Take graham crackers
Chocolate and marshmallows too
Meet them together
That's all you do

Gooey, yummy
So many to eat
A perfect night
A perfect treat

Gaze at the sky,
For a falling star
Try to count
How many there are

Morning has come
We must pack our gear
A promise we made
To come next year

Remember the s'mores
That I made
Here is the recipe
For you to take

Ellen Grape's Special S'mores

Ingredients

1 graham cracker

½ chocolate candy bar

1 large marshmallow

Break a long graham cracker in half, making two squares. Place half of the chocolate bar on top of the cracker. Place the marshmallow on a skewer on stick. This is where mom or dad takes over to roast the marshmallow. Remember safety is always first. Once it is golden brown, let them remove the marshmallow and place on top of the chocolate bar. All you have to do now is squish it down with the other graham cracker piece.

What makes mine so special you ask? I add caramel syrup and sprinkles on top, take a bite, it's hard to stop!! Mmmmm, give me smore!!!

Make them camping
Make them at home
Always make plenty
All will be gone

Thank you for coming
Time went by fast
I treasure our friendship
That forever will last

Your Friend,

Ellen Grape

Printed in the United States
by Baker & Taylor Publisher Services